Tanvi's Birthday

Yuma Vasuki
Translation: S. Pavani | R.S. Rehana Sulthana

Tanvi's Birthday
Yuma Vasuki
Translation: S. Pavani | R.S. Rehana Sulthana
First Published: August, 2023

Published by

BOOKS FOR CHILDREN
Imprint of Bharathi Puthakalayam
7, Elango Salai, Teynampet, Chennai - 600 018
044 -24332424, 24332924, 24339024
Email: bharathiputhakalayam@gmail.com
www.thamizhbooks.com

Foreword

The statement "Writers make national literature, while translators make universal literature" holds true as translation is considered to be the most intricate of all intellectual endeavours. I express my sincere gratitude to the faculty members of the Postgraduate and Research Department of English at Justice Basheer Ahmed Sayeed College for Women for taking the initiative to encourage young minds to funnel their passion towards the art of translation.

The translation of Yuma Vasuki's Thanviyin Pirandha Naal from Tamil to English, undertaken by undergraduate students as part of their research project is a praiseworthy work of art. I extend my heartfelt congratulations to the Department of English for guiding the younger generation in the right direction and wish them all success.

Dr. N. Mehar Taj
Associate Professor & Head
PG & Research Department of English
Justice Basheer Ahmed Sayeed College for Women
(Autonomous), Chennai-18

Acknowledgement

We wish to register our profound gratitude to the Almighty for guiding us at every stage of life. We would like to extend special thanks to our parents who were the source of success in our lives.

We would like to place on record our sincere thanks to Thiru. Yuma Vasuki, a renowned writer for permitting us to translate his book ThanviyinPirandhaNaal.

We would like to thank profoundly the Multi-disciplinary Research Centre, Justice Basheer Ahmed Sayeed College for Women for giving us this golden opportunity to work on this project titled The Nuances of Translation. We are also deeply indebted to Dr. N. Mehar Taj, the Head, Department of English for her invaluable support and guidance in completing this project.

Our sincere thanks to our class teachers, Mrs. K. Pahlavi Mustafa, & Ms. Anis Fathima Faisal who were the pillars of support at every stage.

"Anything is possible when you have the right people to support you". We are immensely grateful to our friends & family for their active support and encouragement.

Last but not the least we thank each other for completing this journey of translation with a great spirit.

After a journey full of rain and storm, we are finally looking forward to a rainbow. We would sincerely hope that this journey will continue by the grace of Almighty.

Content

1
Tanvi's Birthday

It was five in the morning when little Tanvi was in her dreamland. It was her birthday, so her parents got up at 3 in the morning and started preparing for her birthday celebration. After finishing the work, they both sat near her bed and were waiting for her to wake up. Meanwhile, they were discussing about the party in a soft voice since Tanvi was still sleeping.

Tanvi turned over and slept. She left a sigh. At that time, a miracle happened which we had never seen or heard before. Do you know what it is?

From her sigh, a sparrow appeared with its flapping wings. With her next breath, a little elephant appeared which jumped and ran with excitement.

With the release of her next breath, a puppy came and made a somersault and danced.

From the successive breaths released from Tanvi, fruit lending trees, animals, birds, flower garden, forest, rainbow, rain, summer, snow, sky, stars, sun, moon, mountains, sea, bushes, song, painting and everything appeared.

First, a peacock came. It spread its plumage and danced happily. Its plumage shown brightly in the sunlight. While dancing it said, "Come my friends, today is our dear little girl Tanvi's birthday, and we should gather and discuss the gifts that we can give her on this day. Come!"

Then appeared a waterfall. It was falling from a high distant mountain, with a clattering sound on the pebbles. It said with exitement:

"I love Tanvi a lot. She has sunk into and, played, swam and bathed with me several times. She loved me very much. She loves my beauty and my green surroundings. But they destroyed the mountain and built buildings there. After that the mountain and I died. But in Tanvi's mind, I am still flowing with a clattering sound like before. Tanvi is a lover of nature. I wish to kiss her sincerely, on this birthday of hers.

Next came a big lion and spoke.

"Once Tanvi came to the animal exhibition with her father and mother. with desire and love, she looked at all the animals. At that time, I was very sick in my cage. I also got a sore on my right front leg and it hurted badly. I sat down licking my sore and cried uncontrollably out of pain. From outside the cage, Tanvi saw me and worried a lot. As I was unable to walk, she kept looking at me worriedly for a long time. At that time, she did not know how to heal my pain. A few days later I died. But Tanvi still thinks about me. In her mind, I'm still roaming in the forest as a healthy and strong lion. So, I too wish to kiss that dear little girl.

Then a voice was heard. It was the voice of the forest. Which said:

"Once Tanvi came to me. She danced among the plants and enjoyed herself. She swung on the wild vines, hanging from the big trees. She collected various flowers, made bouquets and gifted them to her friends. She enjoyed watching many birds. She ran along with butterflies and dragonflies.I used to be her great lovable forest. But now I am no more. They destroyed me and built a factory in the place where I used lived. But in her mind, I'm still living in the same forest. I will be happy if I can give her a loving kiss."

Suddenly, "I too have to speak about Tanvi!" a voice exclaimed. It was the voice of the fields. "During holidays, Tanvi used to spend more time in fields. She was interested in watching the growth of the crops. She also helped farmers when they planted and harvested the crops. Now they have cleared the fields and had constructed houses. But in her mind, she thinks that I'm still the same green field. I too wish to kiss her on her birthday. But I don't know the way to do it."

"She likes to watch the sunrise and the sunset. I too would like to kiss her," said the sun.

Immediately the moon said with anger, the moon said, "How often she used to sit with her friends near the door and eat the food by watching the moon. In full moonlight, she often plays! I too want to kiss her.

"Everyone be quiet" the sparrow declared. "You all don't know. Once an eagle caught me. Somehow, I escaped from its mouth and fell from a great height. My left leg was injured. Only Tanvi took me and saved me. She fed me, applied medicine for my wound and cured me. From there on, I lived for a long time and then died. But to her mind, I am still flying. On her birthday, I will surely kiss her."

All of them wanted to kiss Tanvi. How is this possible?

At that time, Art, music and dance discussed altogether and arrived at a conclusion.

"Ok, we all love Tanvi. Tanvi is good at painting, singing and dancing as well. She has a good place in her heart for us. So, follow whatever we say. Let all of our wishes join together and become a single rose. Let it bloom outside Tanvi's window. When she wakes up, the beauty of our thoughts will never not fail to fascinate her. She will come and smell the rose. Then we can offer her our kisses!"

Everyone loved this idea.

Then, do you know what happened?

When Tanvi took her breath in, one by one everything went into her heart. When she woke up, at first, she saw the marvellous rose which has bloomed beautyfully outside her window.

While her wished her saying, uttered "Happy Birthday Tanvi!", she smiled at them and ran towards the rose. She doesn't know that how such a wonderful rose bloomed near her home. Even to her mother and father, it seemed a wonder.

Tanvi, slowly sat near the rose, smelled it which was full of dew drops. Wow! What a good fragrance! No one in the world would have smelt such a good fragrance, Tanvi felt. Without her knowledge, she bent down and kissed the rose.

Meanwhile, "Our most lovable girl Tanvi, Happy Birthday to you!" was uttered by everything and Do you know what are all the ones who kissed her? Air, shells, fields, forests, mountains, plants, rivers, animals and everything! everything!

2
Was What Jai did right?

Mom was working on something with her laptop on the table and she was having a headache. She massaged her forehead with her fingers. She thought that it would be so nice to drink some hot tea. She got up and opened the fridge and found that there was no milk.

"JAI", looking out the window at the street, she called out loudly.

Jai was sitting on the bed, leaning against the wall. He was reading a story book. "Here I come, mom!" he said and ran to his mother.

The ginger cat, his pet, ran behind him.

"Oh! Are you here? I thought you were playing in the street. Okay, Will you go to the tea shop at the end of the street and buy a cup of tea for me. I got headache." she asked her son.

"Okay, Ma." said Jai.

His mother gave him money and flask for the tea. Jai kept the flask in the front basket of his bicycle and set off to the shop.

Then, his cat meowed as if it is saying, "I too want to join, my captain.

Wait for me!!!"

Jai looked back hearing his cat's voice, "MEOW". He lifted the ginger cat and made it sit in the front basket. The bicycle took off.

The cat turned its head and looked around curiously.

How did the cat get the name Ginger CAT?

Jai only named the cat because it is copper in colour. Similarly, the ginger cat would also call Jai as 'CAPTAIN'. What is the reason for this?

One day the ginger cat was sitting on the couch and was watching television with Jai. Then there was scene of a political procession.

Everyone in the procession held up one's portrait and chanted, 'LONG LIVE THE CAPTAIN!!! LONG LIVE THE CAPTAIN!!" Even though the cat did not know the meaning, the word "Captain" caught its attention and it seemed to like the word. So, the ginger cat came to a conclusion that 'If everyone in the procession keeps shouting 'Captain, captain.' then it must be a great word.'

From that day, it started calling its owner and its beloved friend as "CAPTAIN" with love and affection.

But whatever it calls, whatever word it may utter, we will hear it as just, 'Meow'. Poor ginger cat!!! Jai would be more than happy to have his cat call him 'Captain', Wouldn't he??? But there is no way for it to happen.

Salambhai's tea shop is not crowded. There is always a crowd of tea lovers in his shop. His tea has such a rich and rare taste. People would come from far of places in two-wheelers to drink his tea.

"Give me a parcel of tea, bhai!" Jai said and held out the flask and the money. He also added, "Wash the flask well in the hot water!!"

At that time, his cat jumped down from the bicycle basket and said, "Give good tea to my Captain Jai, bhai. Otherwise, his name will be damaged in our home," it warned.

Salam Bhai smiled kindly at the cat, which looked up at him and said, "Meow, meow." He took the flask and the money and said:

"Come Jai. You are just in time. The store is about to run out of tea powder. Can you go to the Johnson shop and buy one kilo of Rabbit tea powder?"

Jai did not deny it. "I will buy it, bhai" he offered to help. He took the money from bhai and left with his ginger cat.

The Johnson grocery store is three streets away. Jai's mom does her grocery shopping there.

The ginger cat likes bicycle rides. Jai has arranged a basket to take his cat, to take it with him wherever he goes. The ginger cat looked around with amusement as it meowed slowly and softly. It sounded like a song to its owner Jai. He gripped the handlebar with one hand and with the other hand, he patted his cat. Then the cycle stumbled down slightly. The frightened cat advised Jai, "Captain Jai, ride the cycle carefully, avoid accidents!!"

Six to seven people were standing in Johnson's shop buying things. Johnson smiled at Jai as he got down the bicycle.

"Uncle, Salambai asked me to get a packet of Rabbit tea powder," said Jai. He stood up and held out the money.

Taking the money, Johnson said, "Jai, do me a favour. Today is my daughter's birthday. I have placed a cake order at Modern Bakery. Just now they informed me that the cake is ready and they asked me to come and get it. The store is crowded, so I cannot go. Can you go and get it?"

Without hesitation, Jai accepted and said, "Okay uncle. I will go and get it"

His daughter Jayaseeli is Jai's friend. She is a sixth-grade student in his school. She likes Jai, who is studying in the seventh standard. She loves to eat lunch with him at school. Sometimes she asks Jai, "Mom won't come to pick me up after school in the evening. Shall I go with you in your cycle?"

Whenever she comes together like that, she sits in the back carrier and asks him riddles that she created on her own. If she asks ten to fifteen riddles, he will answer rightly only six or seven. She reads lot of books in the school library.

Modern Bakery is located in the center of the town near the Clock Tower. It's bit far. Jai needs to pass through the crowded market streets.

Jai slowly and carefully rode all the way. The ginger cat sat on the front basket and looked around happily and enthusiastically.

There were only one or two people in the Modern Bakery. When he stopped his cycle in front of the bakery, his cat jumped down.

Bakery's owner Ishaki sir is also someone who Jai knows. He is one of the close friends of Jai's father. His son Muniyan is also studying with Jai in the same class. Muniyan is talented in playing chess. Last year he won the state level chess competition that was held between the high schools. That beautiful cup is now kept in the small wooden shelf of the headmaster's room. Like mirror it reflects one's face perfectly.

As soon as Ishaki uncle saw Jai he smiled and welcomed him.

"Come, Jai! What's the matter?"

"Hello, Uncle. Johnson uncle told me to get the cake".

Ishaki got the cash given by Jai and gave him a medical prescription.

"Jai, you have come this long why don't you do me a favor and go. Please get me the medicines in the slip and then go."

Jai immediately said: "I'll buy and come uncle!".

Medical shop is located at the right-side shore of the lotus lake. One should pass by the Municipal Office. Or, to reach sooner via a short cut one should go by the girls' high school. Jai chose to go by the latter one.

The lady who runs the medical shop has lost her right leg in an accident. She and Jai's mother are college friends.

"Come, Jai. What's the matter? How are your parents?" enquired the lady.

"They are good, aunty! Ishaki uncle has told me to buy all these medicines." Jai replied

Jai gave the cash and the prescription.

"Okay, I'll bring them. While coming I forgot to bring my food dear. Can you buy me a sambar rice and go?"

"Okay, aunty! I'll buy and come!". Jai kindly accepted to help.

Now the ginger cat severely opposed Jai. "Boss Jai, if we keep on doing work for everyone when can we go home and give mom her tea?"

Aunt looked at the red cat weirdly and said:

"Why is this cat shouting like that? Is it hungry? While going home I'll get a packet of biscuit for him."

Jai got on the cycle after getting the money from the aunt.

There is a big food mess in the next street. But the prices are high. Moreover, the food items won't even taste good. There is another food mess near the bus stop which is pretty good mess and the price is also reasonable. Jai went there.

It's just a five minutes distance. But the pathway was under new road construction, therefore he was forced to take the long route.

By the time he brought the food for his aunt, half an hour went by.

"Thanks a lot, dear! You've come at the right time!" said aunt and handed him the medicines and the balance amount in a paper bag.

Ishaki sir was working busily in the bakery. He got the medicines from Jai and Then he gave him a huge cake and the balance amount.

In Johnson uncle's grocery shop, there was no one now. He was relaxed and was reading the newspaper after having lunch. He got the cake and the change which jai gave and said:

"I have informed your Dad Jai. You must come to Jaiseeli's birthday party with your parents. Also bring this cat. The cat too will get biriyani."

Jai started his journey to Salam bhai's shop after getting the two-rabbit tea powder.

It seemed as if Salam bhai was waiting for him. He hurriedly got the tea powder and transferred it to a tin.

He filled Jai's flask with tea, closed it tightly and gave it to him.

It was two hours since he left the house. The ginger cat which is now sitting in the front basket of the cycle gave no sound and was all calm.

As soon as Jai stopped the cycle in front of his house the cat jumped, ran inside the house and hid.

Jai brought the flask and kept it on the table. Mother was working in the kitchen. She was scowling. Jai understood that she is very angry with him. He himself poured the tea into a glass and kindly gave it to her.

"I don't want tea or anything, Go! Will it take two hours to get a tea from the shop at the end of this street. Nowadays you have become spoilt unlike before. You have roamed around, played nicely and now coming and standing here! Why would I need this tea now? You can drink it yourself, just Go!" said mother furiously.

Jai got scared. He felt sad. With a lot of hesitation, he started:

"No mom, I went to Salam bhai's shop right, then he…"

Mother stopped him and warned,

"You don't have to explain anything. You are going to lie to hide your mistake, right? Shut up!"

There came the ginger cat from below the bed and started to shout loudly: "Don't blame Captain Jai! I can't bear the injustice done to him!"

But mother looked at the cat with a look of confusion that why the cat is shouting like that.

Father who came inside, saw the tea glass on the table.

"Oh, oh! I came home thinking to ask for a glass of tea. Here the tea is ready!" said father and drank the tea. "It's good but it's a little less hot!" he said and kept the glass down.

Jai felt happy. Even the ginger cat praised his father: "Meow! Meow!"

"I have some work. You guys eat. I'll eat after sometime" saying that father, went inside the room and sat with his laptop open.

"Bring your plate!" said mother.

Jai got his plate and kept it on the dining table. The ginger cat got its yellow-colored plate and sat on the floor.

Mother served the food. Jai insilence was observing her face. Mother's anger did not fade yet. while eating, Ginger cat saw mother's face and then Jai's face. Mother who always serves the food happily, served it with a gloomy face today which made the cat upset.

Those who are reading this can say, whether was, is Jai really wrong or not.

3
How did the little dog get its name?

What hurts the little dog more is that: it does not have a name. Only Dogs that are grown in the houses are given names. This is something that we all know right? Who will name the dogs that are roaming in the streets? That little dog does not have anyone. It's been two months since its mother died. Maybe there is a chance that this puppy will get a name before this story ends.

The market near the street had three moving shops. People will be crowded in the morning for breakfast. The fishes caught on the other side of the market would also be brought here for sale.

The breakfast for the mother dog and the little dog would be the leftover food thrown by the people. The little dog likes the spicy chutney and masala mix very much compared to the left over idly or dosa pieces.

"Dear, you should not consume spicy food. It will cause diarrhea" warned the mamma dog. But still the little one could not restrict itself from eating them.

As usual the mamma dog, along with the little one went to the place where they get their food. Standing on one side of the road it saw the leftover food on the banana leaves on the opposite side of the road. The leftover food could be seen clearly between the leaves. The mamma dog was so happy. It turned around, looked at little dog and barked softly.

What is the meaning behind its bark?

We say words like 'Okay!', 'Very Good!', 'Follow Me', 'Come on', 'Hurry up!', it should be something like that.

Just then came, an unexpected interference!

The Mamma dog saw the other dogs running towards the food lying on the other side of the road. That's all it took for the mamma dog to get alert. With that thought of taking the food before the other dogs could reach, it

rushed to the other side of the road. Tch, tch. Poor thing!

The dog got stuck in the front wheel of the garbage truck that came with high speed on the road at the same time. The screech from the mamma dog was heard and the truck halted suddenly.

From that truck came down a sanitary worker, and he saw under the wheels. Blood was oozing out of the mouth of the dead mamma dog which was thrown into the truck. Again, the truck sped up. Who would have expected such a thing to happen.

It took some time for the little dog to understand what had happened. Just after everything was over it rushed and ran behind the truck, chasing it. It could not run after a certain distance. The truck vanished from the sight.

After that, the existence itself became a tough thing for the little dog. Huge dogs would come and consume the food found at near the market place. If at all the little dog went near, they would show their fangs and would shoo it away, scaring it. Can rabbits fight the wolf and win them? This is also something similar to that. Because of this the little dog had to search for food elsewhere.

Not even once it would get food to fill its stomach. When it felt hunger, it would go to the people standing near the shops.

It will touch their legs, keep its face sad, will beg them to buy something. Majority of them will move away. One or two will buy something and feed it.

When there was no way for food, with unbearable hunger it would lie in some corner of a road, thinking about its mother and cry. If it had its mother with him, he wouldn't have been hit by the terrible hunger.

At such times, the little dog would see the other dogs being taken on the side of the road in a collar chain. Few dogs would be covered with fur, few others would be without any fur but their body shined like a mirror. The dog owner order them: "Brownie, come this side!'," Blacky, don't run, stop!", "Scooby, enough let's go, come!".

When the owners talk with their dogs by calling out their names, it would be fascinating for the little dog. The little dog started to yearn for its own name.

The dogs that were brought in collar chains would see the skinny, hungry little dog sitting in the corner with disgust. In a way to scare it or to mock it, they would growl and grunt. They will try to pounce on the little dog. One among them barked looking at the little dog: "Hey! Beggar dog, how dare you sit in the same street that we go! Get away from here immediately!" The little dog would think, as runs away with horror and terror. "Ain't I a dog too? Then why are they all so hostile towards me? What harm have I done to them?"

One day, the little dog was curled up at one such corner of a street. A car stopped next to it. The driver got down and went to the next shop to buy something. The little dog noticed then, that a huge dog was looking at it through the window of the next seat to the drivers.

The dog was black in color, with shiny body and twinkling eyes, said to the little dog after observing it: "Greetings, little friend. You look like someone who is suffering from hunger. Don't worry. Your time will come. Have faith!. Even I used to be

a street dog once. Just like you, suffering from hunger and lying on the road, a man pitied me. He took me with him. The one who drove the car, that person. Today I have no worries!"

After saying this, that dog picked up a packet of bread from the car with the help of its paws and threw it out. At the same time four huge dogs barked and pounced on the packet. They had a fight among them on who would get the packet.

There was a total mess!!!

The little dog ran away in fear! and It kept running.

It ran searching for a safe place and ended up near a river bank, And then it's fear went away. But it became too tired because of running. Stumbling and shaking, it reached a bush and fainted between them.

Jai was coming that way after school. In the morning he goes to school using the main road and, in the evening, while returning from the school he uses this pathway. In this way, there will not be so much traffic. Children could be seen playing in the doorways of lakeside cottages. The bushes on the riverbank could be seen swaying in the air, in the middle of the lake, the fishermen could be seen on their boats. One can enjoy watching these things while going through this street.

One such evening, Jai was walking along the shore happily. A woodpecker suddenly flew from the nearby tree. He was happy on seeing it. A herd of ducks were swimming to the shore after playing in the river.

Jai walked whistling happily. He felt like singing. Would you also feel like singing while walking in such a beautiful surrounding?

He started to sing loudly: "if the heart grows will the world grow,

Therefore humans…"

Then suddenly he heard a sound from a nearby bush "bow, wow!". It startled Jai, his heart stopped for a second. Jai ran away in fear, thinking that a dog was coming to bite him. At the same time, the little dog ran away in the opposite direction thinking that someone is coming to attack it. Jai ran to a certain distance and then stopped, turned and looked back 'Oh, oh. Did I run away fearing for this pitiful dog's bark,' laughed Jai. Little dog too stopped after running a certain distance and looked back 'Oh, oh. Did I fear hearing this good boy's voice' thought the little dog, wagging its tail.

He signalled to the little dog to come near him using his hands. The little dog did not hesitate nor did it think. It touched his legs and looked up at him with longing. Jai understood. He sat, kneeling down. He tore a plain paper from his note book which he took out. He took his tiffin box and took the two uneaten tortillas tore them into pieces and kept them on the paper. The little dog enthusiastically ate them, wagging its tail.

Jai waited till it finished eating and then signalled it to follow him. It understood. He walked in front, the little dog followed him. Jai jumped in happiness and continued to sing while walking. The little dog jumped with joy and started singing,

"I am good among the dogs!

I am waiting to do good –

Who will protect me in this world –

Who will name me among the humans!"

Jai laughed upon hearing the little dogs sound. The little dog started to sing more enthusiastically thinking that Jai had understood it and hence laughing at it.

Father was reading newspaper while sitting on the easy chair in front of the house. Next to his father sat his mother on a chair, working on in her laptop. Jai feared his father's reaction upon seeing the little dog. Hopefully mother will manage stating 'Let it be with us'. But father might get angry.

His Father saw him standing near the entrance gate. When he opened the door, he saw the little dog coming behind Jai. He raised his eyebrows. He glared at it after removing his glasses.

Right then, Jai told his father with utmost obedience: "This dog is so poor dad. It is very weak. I brought it so that it can grow with us".

Mother saw that dog and gave a kind smile. He too wagged his tail upon seeing mother. Dad shouted after folding his newspaper: "First go and leave this dog outside, Ugly!" said he, suddenly moving his hands indicating the entrance.

With the force that he shook his hands, his glass flew off went and landed near the entrance door. Thank God, it did not break. Just see what the poor little dog did! You will be surprised!

It immediately jumped and graped the glass and came back. It kept the glass near his father, touched his legs with its stout and looked up with longing. His Father, who earnestly looked at the dog for some time started to smile unknowingly. Mother laughed aloud on seeing this.

"Okay, okay, Go. First give it a bath!" said his father and continued reading his newspaper.

"Come Tommy, let's go!" called Jai. The little dog came to know its name then. It was immensely happy. It jumped with excitement.

"There came a friend,

Who gave me a good name!" sang the little dog.

That's how the little dog got its name. Above all, it got a good life. Hereafter, we need not worry about the little dog.

4
Thanvi's Garden

Little Thanvi was returning home from school. There was a house with a terrace at the beginning of a small street, leading back to the house from the main street. In front of the house, a Periwinkle plant with its shiny leaves and a lot of pretty flowers caught our Thanvi's attention. The dark blue coloured flowers that bloomed in clusters were further embellished by the of summer evening Sun.

Today she couldn't get past those flowers. She forgot the world and was mesmerized by the beauty of those flowers. She bent down and touched the flowers with her little hands.

To her surprise, the door opened suddenly!!! and the man who appeared shouted at her asking, "Why are you trying to pluck the flowers?"

Thanvi was too stunned to speak. "Don't be scared. Why do you want this plant?" asked the man.

"Thought that it would be nice to plant it in my home" Thanvi replied in a slow voice.

The man asked her to come the next day.

The following day, our Thanvi went to that house. Just as he assured, he had plucked 15 plants and kept it ready for her.

Thanvi delightfully thanked him and went back to her house.

Within two months, Thanvi's entrance looked like a little garden. The small plant has grown so big and the branches started growing quickly. Little Thanvi made sure to water the plants every day. The plant was full of pretty flowers.

Thanvi's dad bought many such plants like Rose, jasmine, hibiscus, tropical flame plants and this made her garden grow more blissfully. Thanvi enjoyed studying in the veranda while looking at her lovely garden. Her teacher heard about this and in fact visited her house. Her teacher was happy on the sight of the flowers and she praised Thanvi. Little Thanvi was so proud of herself.

This happy journey continued until an unexpected problem popped up. It was a Sunday afternoon, and the Sun was out and playing. The situation in the garden was quite out of the blue. There was a dog lying between those periwinkle flowers. As a result of this, four pretty periwinkle plants were crushed and smashed.

Thanvi was so shocked when she saw what had happened.

Poor little girl got angry and drove away the dog saying, "RUN!!!! YOU DOG!!!!! DON'T EVER COME HERE!!!"

The dog ran away. Thanvi couldn't believe what has happened and she couldn't accept the fact.

This did not end right there. Every morning Thanvi started watering the plants. As soon as the day's temperature rose the dog will come and lie in between the plants by digging a hole. Upon seeing this Thanvi got furious and shooed the dog away. The dog went away for short while but returned back to the same place. This went on for a few days.

How to save these plants from the dog was the only thought that was going on in Thanvi's mind all the time at home and at school as well.

Sadness prevailed on seeing the dog spoiling the plants day by day and all that she could do is to watch it helplessly.

One afternoon, as Thanvi was studying in the hall her mother was working in the kitchen. Suddenly she saw her mother emerging hurriedly from the kitchen. She came and stood under the fan in the hall. Since there was no fan in the kitchen. Her mother was sweating heavily, her face and hands were totally covered in sweat.

She wiped her sweat with the towel while muttering to herself about not being able to bear the heat. After sometime she went back into the kitchen to cook but she again hurried into the hall to stand under the fan. This happened almost 4 times till she completed her cooking.

Thanvi felt sorry for seeing her mother in such a condition. She seemed to look dull and tired due to the heat and excessive sweating. On seeing her mother's present state she was suddenly reminded of something.

At that time, Thanvi looked outside her window, and saw the dog lying in its usual place.But this time Thanvi was not angry.

After coming to a conclusion Thanvi filled a bucket with water and brought it to the front yard of her home. On seeing Thanvi, the dog moved away and stared at her from a distance. The dog saw Thanvi from a distance.

Thanvi poured the water under a moringa tree that was placed on the left side of her house. After pouring the water she looked at the dog and said, ' from now on you should lie in this place, see, here...here...' said Thanvi pointing out to that place. She made lot of signs and also used expressions to make the dog understand what she was trying to say. But Thanvi was doubtful whether she has succeeded in this regard.

Few days later, to her surprise she saw the dog lying in the position that Thanvi pointed out that day under the moringa tree.

Thanvi felt elevated upon seeing this. She immediately went inside the kitchen, took a plate of food and fed the dog. It finished the food within a few minutes. From then onwards, feeding the dog became a daily routine for Thanvi and even the dog stopped spoiling the plants by lying in between the plants.

The dog started to live there. It followed her everyday to school, accompanied her till the street end and, in the evening, it waited for her in the same place. Upon Thanvi's arrival both will go to a nearby shop where Thanvi used to buy snacks and candies and both will eat together. After this both went back home together.

5
Counting

The Sun has already risen when Thanvi came out with a big bowl. The ginger cat which accompanied her looked up at the sky and meowed. The entire street was wet from the last night's rain. Some water stagnated here and there. Her daffodils plant was beautifully reflecting the stagnant water at the door step. Because of the rain, she need not water that plant for some days.

Thanvi looked at the Daffodil plant. The plant was slightly bent down due to the rain. The lovely smile she used to have every morning when she saw her daffodil plant, lit up her face, today too.

The Flowers beautifully bloomed on the plant. They were red daffodils with the pink colour at the edge of the petals, and the red colour at the base. The rain drops were still present on the leaves and the flowers, and were dripping from time to time.

Thanvi then started to pluck the flowers. She plucked the flowers that were too high for her to reach, by slightly bending the branch. That day, there seemed to be about a hundred or a hundred and fifty flowers bloomed on the plant. Suddenly she thought, "Oh, I can count it and see!!"

Then she started counting as she was plucking the flowers and put them into the bowl.

"One… two… ten… twenty-three…"

She suddenly noticed a big drop of water, which was hanging on a flower and was shining like a diamond in the sunlight. WOW!!!! How beautiful!!! When she looked closely, she could see the reflection of her face and the surrounding objects in that drop!!! It was an ecstatic moment for Thanvi. How rare it is!!! Mesmerized by the beauty of the rain drop, Thanvi got lost at its sight for a while. A sudden gust of wind blew, the rain drop began to fall from the flower and immediately Thanvi caught it in her palm. The gentle chillness spread over her hand and thrilled her.

Then, suddenly she remembered that she was counting the flowers. She failed to remember where she lost the count….

It seemed that morning, the sun has arrived earlier. That was good too. All the flowers would bloom well, only when the sun shines. Thanvi came out with the bowl. The ginger cat that came along with Thanvi, sneaked behind her on seeing the dog from the opposite house. She came and stood near the plant. There seemed to be more flowers today than usual. We will know how many flowers had bloomed, if we count them.

This time, Thanvi began to pluck the flowers by counting them carefully. "One…. sixteen…. Twenty-seven…."

At that moment, she saw a miracle. A yellow butterfly sat on a flower. It was a bright lemon-yellow colour!!! The more she saw it, the more she got excited. Acording to Tanvi, butterfly sitting on her flower was a huge happening. She welcomed the butterfly sweetly saying, "Come, come!! only now you found the way to come here??" Innocent Thanvi was afraid that if she continues to pluck the flowers, the plant would shake and as a result the butterfly would fly away.

The red flowers, green leaves with a yellow butterfly as a background looked amazing. She wanted to see this beautiful sight for some more time. The butterfly was looking at her with its two delicate blacks dot like eyes on its yellow head. When she turned to her mother's calling from inside, the butterfly flew away.

Thanvi again lost her count....

Then one morning when Thanvi came to pick the flowers, the snow had not cleared yet. She felt a slight chill. She breathed the fresh smell of the dew-drenched grass and plants. Her cat was rolling on the grass, playing happily.

Today, there were only a few flowers that bloomed on the daffodil plant. Each flower was covered with snowdrops. The cold and the wind cheered her up. She was firm that she must finish counting the flowers today.

She started counting as she plucked the flowers. "One.... Eleven... thirty-six...."

While counting, a small green coloured worm present in the lower stem of the daffodil plant, caught her attention. By taking a closer look, she could find its delicate fur. It was moving slowly. Where did this beautiful worm come from? Is this an immature worm? Where is it going? She was thinking about all these, while looking at the worm. Suddenly the small worm disappeared!!!

Thanvi was startled!! Where is the worm???

It was only later when she looked here and there, she found that there was a chameleon on the same branch as the worm!!

It was the one that stretched out its tongue and ate the worm.

You could find the chameleon, only when you look closely. The colour of the plant was the same as its own. It looked at her, by closing and opening its mouth very slowly, with its tail curled up. Amazed Thanvi, laughed at its sad look which was so pitiful. Then the chameleon started moving slowly. It was at that moment when Thanvi was watching where it was heading to, she remembered that she had missed the count....

That morning, when Thanvi woke up, she was so stubborn that no matter what, she must finish counting the flowers which bloomed on the daffodil plant, without fail!!!!!!!

It was cloudy, when she came out with the bowl. It was a dark morning without the sun. The daffodil flowers were not fully bloomed. It would have bloomed beautifully if it was sunny. But there were enough bloomed daffodils.

She plucked the flowers as she counted them and collected them in the bowl. "One…. Eighteen… forty-six…"

That moment, she heard a sound that went like "eeeeiiuu!!" It was the sound of a peacock. Peacock often came to the farm next to Thanvi's home.

Thanvi suddenly turned to that side to see if the peacock was visible.

There, she noticed a huge rainbow which appeared in the lower sky!!! its colours looked clear and bright. Thanvi had never seen anything like that before! What a miraculous sight!! Thanvi's eyes widened at the beautiful sight. Forgetting everything around her, she was astonished at the beauty of the rainbow. Then the peacock flew across the rainbow and sat on the top of a tall palm tree with the sound of "eeeiiuu".

She was looking at the rainbow for such long time, forgetting herself completely. She came to her senses only when her cat rubbed her leg, realizing that she missed her count…

The next time she was counting the flowers, the sparrows came and disturbed her. Another time, few dragon flies came and sat on the leaves and thwarted her attempts. The other time when she started her counting, the buzzing of little black bees stopped her from counting further.

She tried counting the flowers in her daffodil plant every day. But she was never able to finish counting the flowers. Because, miracles were always happening around her.

6
Gift

In the morning, they heard the sound of goats bleating, "MME… MME…" Jai and Thanvi who were studying in the house, peeked at the door. As usual, there stood, three big white goats and two black goats arrived. They were the goats raised by an old lady who lived a few houses away.

……..

One day, at the time when the goats were coming, Jai and Thanvi brought the leftover food from the previous night. They happily ate and left. From that day, every morning, the goats would stand at their door and ask for food, as soon as their stable is opened. Jai and Thanvi collected all the leftover food from the kitchen, put it in a large vessel and mashed it and kept it at the door. The goats would compete and overtake each other and would finish the food very quickly. The white goat, which was the biggest of all, would try to eat all the food by itself by knocking the others.

They also tried keeping the food separately for each in plastic papers. Even then, the goat that finisher its food first would fight with the next goat for food. So, they let them eat it however they want and kept it with food in the vessel which wasalso easier.

Every morning as the goats ate, there would be chaos at the door. Jai and Thanvi wolud laugh

watching the goats push each other. The goats seemed to like the cooked foods more than the plants. They thought that the big white goat's stomach grew bigger after eating here. The little sparrows came and ate the food that where spilled by the goats while eating.

But after the goats finished eating and went to graze, their doorstep would be destroyed because of the food spilled by them. That is when then mom would starts shouting. "Hey, you children!! if you want to feed the goats, can't you do it out side? Look how bad the doorstep with the rangoli has become!!" Then Thanvi will bring a bucket of water and a broom and would clean the place.

There was also problem in feeding the goats, a little away from their gate. There were two dogs in the area. They come running, baring their teeth frighting the goats away and empty all the food. This was the reason why they fed them at the door and even stood to guard nearby. However, the goats were their favourite.

One day, Jai and Thanvi were going to school. People were standing to buy meat at the roadside meat store. There was only a little meat on the store's cutting board. But a goat was tied next to it. That was the goat that will be slaughtered after the available meat is finished.

The goat intensely stared at Jai and Thanvi. It shook its head as if it was asking them, "Are you good??". It was not aware of what was going to happen to it in a short time. It looked at them with so much love and innocence, as if it wanted to play with them. Thanvi could not bear to see it. Tears started flowing from her eyes. Jai also was devastated. But he did not show it on but consoled his sister. Thanvi did not stop crying till she reached the school. That night, the goat came in her dream and asked her to play with it. Only then they decided to feed the goats in the neighbouring stable.

As the days went by, they developed a personal interest in gathering and mashing the leftovers to provide food for the goats. "Beloved, we the goats have come. Will you give us food?" the goats seemed to ask them at the door with the in beating, "MME. MME..." When they heard this sound, the compassionate brother and sister would start their work.

The leftover rice, stale biscuits, the half of the tea which was left in the glass, chapati pieces, kaaraboondhi, fermented butter milk, rasam, poriyal along with everything which they had, they put in the vessel and mash them. They thought that the goats will be able to eat it easily, only if it is well mashed. While mixing and kneading, these different king of foods, a strange smell would come. Sometimes, they would sneeze because of the strange smell. But the goats have absolutely no problem in eating this. Whatever the food was, they ate it with great involvement. After completing the given food they would pitifully look at them as if asking for more food.

One day, there was no sufficient leftover, but they had to feed five goats. What to do? Thanvi poured a lot of water into the rice and kneaded it by adding ten to fifteen handfuls of raw rice from the rice pot. When she kept it at the doorstep, the goats ate happily. But then a tragedy happened. The goats could not understand the situation and failed to eat silently. The five goats, together chewed and swallowed the rice making the sound "kaduk kaduk.." Mom, who came there hearing the sound, saw the goats eating the raw rice and was shocked. Guessing who did that, she grabbed Thanvi's ears and asked, "Why did you touch the rice pot?" Immediately, Jai managed by saying, "No mom, I was the one who took some rice for the goat." Mother warned them saying, "If you ever do it again, I will peel off your skin."

Recently the big-bellied goat, in an attempt to eat hurriedly, lifted the vessel with its horns. As a result, the vessel overturned over its head and fell, and all the food covered its eyes. The goat was scared that suddenly it could not see and ran away. Other goats ran behind it to eat the food that flowed over it. Seeing this, Jai and Thanvi laughed whole heartedly. Whenever they think of this incident, they laughed.

A strange thing happened a few days earlier. The man in the opposite household, washed his mat and spread it out on the wall outside to let it dry. He did not remove the mat the next day either. The mat flew in the air and fell unfurled onto the street. Then the big-bellied goat came running and sat in the middle of the mat. Despite being chased away by the neighbour, the goat refused to move. It looked haughtily as if it was asking "What is your problem with me sitting so majestically?" and continued sitting there. Then Jai and Thanvi came and grabbed the mat and pulled it away, it got up slowly and reluctantly went away.

The big white goat knocked on the iron gate as if it was asking, "My friends, we are here. Why are you late?". Jai came and said, "We are preparing food for you. Please wait for a few minutes!"

Dad had gone to the field early in the morning because there was planting work to do. Mom had cooked breakfast and was picking vegetables in the backyard garden. Jai and Thanvi watered the plants for a little while. They had finish feeding the goats by then.

They started collecting the leftovers from the previous day. There were a few guests the previous day so there were a little more leftovers than usual. They got two little burnt dosas, a half omelette, three cups of rice, leftover wheat semolina, since dad did not eat last night, five slices of bread, coffee, a piece of halwa left uneaten because it fell on the floor, an old mixture, grinded pancake flour which mom had forgotten, crushed tomatoes, coriander chutney, some salted lemon juice along with some pickles.

Jai and Thanvi put everything in a bowl and mashed it. A strange smell rouse from kneading. Thanvi, who saw the banana skin lying in the corner, ran to fetch it and added it to the mixture. Jai suddenly remembered something and immediately he went and took out a packet of peanuts from his bag. He opened the packet and added it to the food, he brought the peanuts long back but forgot.

"Brother, can we add some sugar to it? The goats will love it", said Thanvi.

"Aiyoo! Don't. There is a little sugar in the jar. If we take from that, mother will know and scold us," Jai said.

After mixing everything together, the food turned into a paste. The goats now have better food than ever before. It was a feast for them. Both the brother and sister were satisfied.

Outside, the goats were making sounds for food, banging on the iron gate. At that moment, Jai had a doubt, "What to do if the goats get diarrhea after eating this mixture of different ingredients?" He also told this to his sister. Thanvi smiled. "Do the goats have stomachs like us? They eat all kinds of plants. This won't affect them." assured Thanvi.

By this time, the goats were shouting loudly and they brought the vessel and kept it outside. The goats started eating busily. Since they hurriedly ate the food, they understood that the goats liked the food. At that time their mom called them: "Hey, children, come here!!"

In the garden, the mother had prepared a plant bed. She fertilized some plants. Jai drew water from the well and poured it into a big bucket. Thanvi used a small bucket to water the plants. After finishing the work, Thanvi started plucking the flowers.

Thanvi plucked many jasmine flowers. There were also many pea flowers. Three yellow roses, one red rose. Besides, she also got ten to sixteen hibiscus flowers. Today she got a big brass bowl full of flowers.

Their mother went to give vegetables to their aunt, who lived in the next street. Jai and Thanvi returned from the garden. The brother was engaged in cleaning the house. The younger sister washed the vessels in the kitchen sink. Then she took the food cooked by her mom along with the plates and kept it in the hall. Now after their mother return, everyone has to eat. Thanvi sat down on the floor and started making a garland with the flowers. Jai was mending some of her book with torn covers.

In no time, Thanvi prepared a beautiful garland. It was a fragrantful and beautiful garland made of jasmine and hibiscus. In between the garland, the blue pea flowers added beauty to it. The roses that were tied at the bottom of the garland made it more beautiful and Jai unconsciously praise the garland, "The garland is very nice, Thanvi!"

Just then a horrible sound came from outside!!! On hearing it, both of them were completely startled. Thanvi got scared so much that she immediately got up and sat next to her brother. The terrible sound was heard again. It sounded like the anguished voice which someone makes when their throat got tightened. It was only when they heard the sound again they understood it was the sound of a goat.

Why did the goat scream so badly? It had never screamed like this before!! What happened?? Did anyone beat it?

The goat was bleating with all its might. Just then, Thanvi remembered what her brother had said while they were kneading food for the goats. It seems that there was a problem with one of the goats not agreeing to the food! That should be the reason! Jai too was thinking similarly with fear.

"Oh my GOD!! We are trapped. What would we do if the goat die because of the food??" cried Jai. Thanvi's eyes were filled with tears. She closed her eyes and folded her hands in prayer: "God, no harm should come to the goat!! Please save it!"

Tears started rolling down her cheeks. Jai wiped her tears and said, "Don't cry Thanvi, don't be afraid, I will take care of it!!!"

Even though he said this, fear was running through him inside. The goat was screaming so loudly as if its life is coming to an end. They didn't know what to do. 'If the goat dies, who will answer that grandma? If dad comes to know of this, it won't matter that much. But if mom comes to know, she will be angry to the point that she will not talk to us for few days.' The fear only increased when they thought about the outcome.

No matter how hard he tried not to cry, tears welled up Jai's eye. His body trembled.

When they heard the cry of the goat once again, they quickly ran and pushed open the closed room door. It opened. Inside the room, their elder brother was sleeping on the bed, propped up against the wall. Their elder brother must have stayed up late at night writing the story. The completed paper was on the table under a paperweight. They flapped gently in the fan air.

Jai came near the bed and softly called, "Lovely brother, lovely brother." There was no movement from his brother. Thanvi tried calling him a little louder. Even then their brother did not wake up. Then the goat screamed aggressively. They immediately grabbed their brother and shook him. "Dear brother, wake up.", Thanvi called crying. Their brother slowly rolled over. He smiled slightly when he saw the two standing near the bed. But when he saw the tears in their eyes, he immediately got up and sat on the bed. Being confused, he got up and washed his face in the wash basin, which was in the corner of the room. Then, Thanvi brought the towel and gave it to him. He wiped his face. After wearing the glasses that Jai took from the writing table, he looked at them. Jai said: "A goat was bleating outside so loudly. It was so scary, brother!!" Thanvi also joined him and said: "Brother, come and have a look at it."

Their brother laughed and said, "Would anyone be afraid of goat's bleating?" and then hugged them. "No brother, please come and look." requested Thanvi and then she pulled him. He put a towel over the vest he was wearing and started walking towards the door. His hands were held tightly by Jai on the left and Thanvi on the right. "Children, why are you scared. I'm here with you right" asked their brother.

The three crossed the porch and came to the veranda. Now the voice of the goat is not heard. It was still quite even after crossing the iron gate. Jai and Thanvi looked around while holding their brother's hands. There were no goats nearby.

Just then, at a distance, they could see the goat herd old lady, sitting under a neem tree. On the sack which was spread beside her, that big-bellied white goat was lying. Their brother brought them there. It was only when they reached there, they understood that the goat had given birth. Now its big belly had gone.

Seeing their brother, the old lady said, "Last time, it gave birth to two, but this time it is only one." The goat was eating the leaves given by the old lady. From time to time, it nervously looked back at its kid. That is when Jai and Thanvi understood the reason behind its big belly. They were seeing the new born kids of the goat for the very first time. "The goat must have been in pain before giving birth. So, it must have called grandmother with a loud sound." said their brother.

The goat's kid was covered with blood. The kid, who had a very small body, tried with a great might to stand up. The mother goat stretched its face eagerly towards its kid. The old lady, while caressing the goat, said very affectionately, "EAT WELL DEAR…. DRINK WATER AFTER EATING…."

Jai and Thanvi were looking at the baby goat with amusement as it was continuously moving around while trying to stand up. Then the old lady asked them, "Do you want this baby? Do you want to raise it?"

Both the little children nodded their heads with an ecstatic smile and said, "Give us this kid grand ma. We will surely take care of it very well. We love this kid so much."

Then the old lady replied, "Okay, let it drink milk from its mother for a few days and grow. Then I myself bring it and give it to you children."

Their elder brother said, "We will pay you grand ma…"

"I don't any need money for this. For a number of days, they have been taking care of the goats by feeding them. Let it be a GIFT for them."

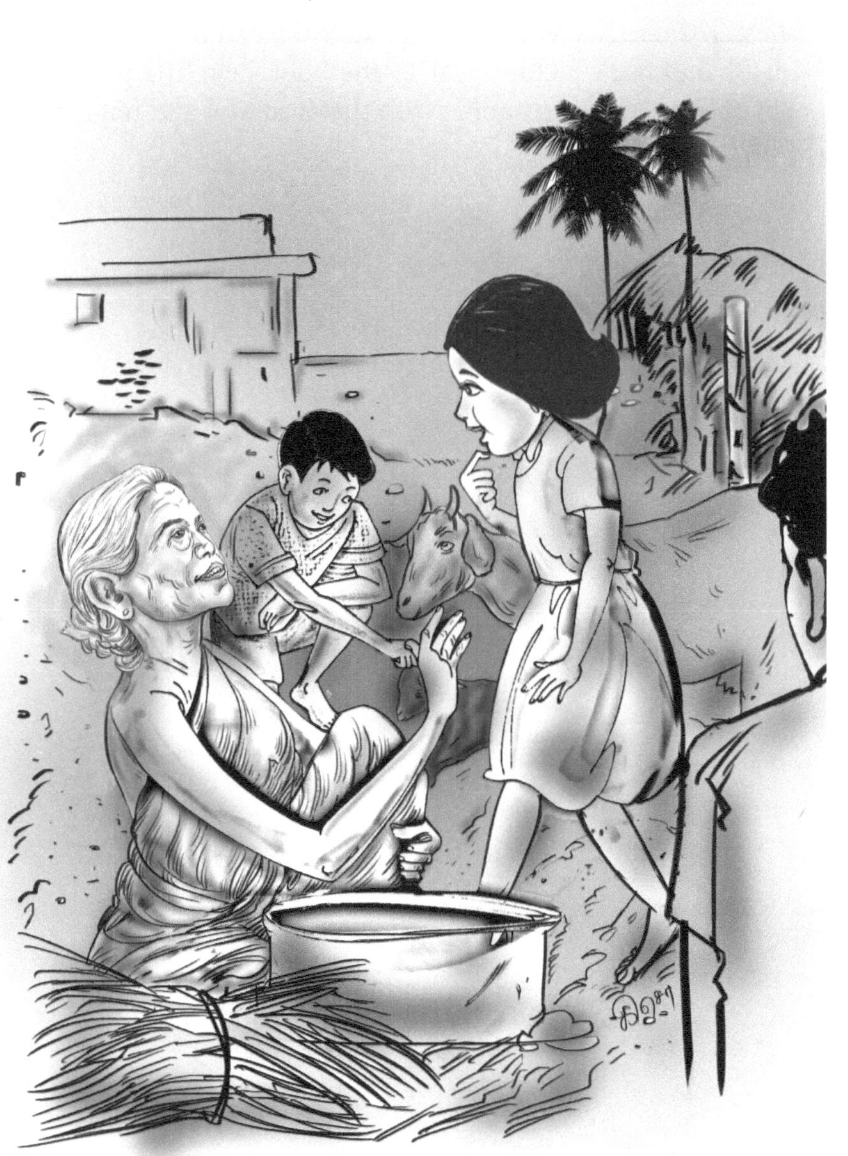

The fear and the agony that they experienced before completely faded away. Jai and Thanvi along with their elder brother came home happily. After they reached, their brother went to take a shower. Then Thanvi took the garland she had made and put it on Bharathiyar's picture next to the bookshelf. The picture of Bharathiyar looked stunning with that beautiful and fragrantful garland.

7
A test written by Gunasundari

As usual, Gunasundari on came to school. time, her father who was affected by polio brought her to school on a hand-operated tricycle. As he lifted her down, he wiped her drooling mouth with his towel. He adjusted the hairpins neatly into the string of jasmine which was falling loose from her head. Then he her kissed on her cheeks and forehead. With a happy smile, she too kissed her father. He waved at her and left.

Guna, kept her wire basket on the floor, in which she bought her food. She took off her book bag from her back. By standing there, she witnessed her father's cycle, until it faded away from the street corner. Only after that, she entered the school.

There were about 800 students studying in that Government Higher Secondary school. Though it was a small school, it looked beautiful.

From that day onwards, Quarterly exams were starting. All the students were busy studying in the last hour. Guna smiled at all those students who were individually studying in the ground and under the big Basil tree.

She was not like other children. She was mentally retarded. She couldn't speak well. When she speaks unclearly and would stutter, her co-students could understand one or two words. Teachers couldn't completely understand her. She was in the state where she was unable to read and write. When teachers teach lessons in the class, all the students will listen, she could be seen scribbling some images in her notebook and would speak something to herself with her drooling mouth. But she was interested in listening to stories.

You know what the was most amazing thingabout her? She knows how to dance! Fascinated by the dance she saw on television, she tries to imitate them to her friends. But she always danced the same type of dance. Standing with both hands on the hips, extend the right leg as if kicking the ball, then the left leg. Then she would spin with outstretched arms, and then suddenly stand up and would jump, and alternately extend the legs. This was her usual dance. At the end, she would bow to mark the end of the show. Teachers and students will clap their hands with great vigoor and shake hands with her to teacher up and

As it was a government school, out of sympathy, she was admitted there in class six. Like other students, free books, notes, uniform and everything else were issued to her. The shoes provided by the school would not fit her. So, her father bought it for her from outside.

She was the darling of the school. All teachers and students were affectionate to her. The headmaster would enquire about her to her father, whenever she failed to turn up. The students and teachers would feel sad if they didn't see her. When she comes the next day, the students and teachers would enquire about her. She will answer all their questions. But they would not understand any of what she says. What mattered to them was the happiness of seeing and talking to her.

She was very close to the science teacher Ramamurthy.

At the time of joining, she was very afraid to come to school. Her father only showered bravery, forced her and brought her and left her every day. Even after coming to school, she would be intimidated by the teachers and students. She would sit huddled in a corner with tears in her eyes.

No one knew how to handle her. The teachers hesitated, fearing that she would cry and make fuss, if they approach her.

Her mother would have tied a handkerchief around her neck to wipe the drool from her mouth. But she doesn't feel like wiping her mouth. If the teachers or students try to wipe, she would run, stand near the locked door and would cry "Daddy… Daddy…"

At that time, Ramamurthy sir, in sixth grade, started to utter stories in his class. during his classes, the other children listened to him with great interest towards his stories, but Guna did not pay head to it. She would be seen gripping the window bars of the classroom and staring out.

Most of the stories uttered by Ramamurthy sir were about birds and animals. He would coo like a cuckoo in the story. He moved like an elephant and lifted his arm like a trunk. Guna slowly began to notice him as he was narrating the story, making noises as a rooster – a cow – a demon – a ghost – a grasshopper – a dog and a cat. Then she started listening to the stories carefully like other children. She also smiled at the others listening to the story, and winced when they remained sad.

After telling stories, Ramamurthy sir would become completely exhausted. He visit would the staff room to drink two or three glasses of water and will take rest by sitting there for a while. He starting telling the stories for Guna and then all the students of the class started listening to him. After that he began telling stories before every class and it became a habit. It was only after Ramamurthy sir started telling stories, Guna became closer to him. After that she started having fun in the class without any fear. From then onwards, she started smiling and laugh with everyone. She ran and played with them. She ate with them in the afternoon.

Whichever class if may be which Ramamurthy sir went to, Guna would follow him and would sit in that class. Whether it is class 7 or class 10. When they saw Guna coming, all the students in their respective classes shouted, "Guna, come and sit by my side!", "Come here Guna, there is place here!" They will compete and welcome her.

Then, from any corner of the class, the snacks would reach her in turns. Peanut candy, murukku,vadai. Sometimes, someone's tiffin box for mid-day meal contains like broad beans fries and masala vadai with cooked rice also arrives. Guna would happily eat whatever was available. Then Ramamurthy sir and children will wipe her mouth. Only after listening to Sir's story before the lesson starts, she goes to her own class. Guna was like his shadow, and followed him to all his classes to listen to his stories. No one stopped her. The teachers thought that she should be happy like this.

All the examination room invigilators went to their allotted examination rooms. The first bell has rung to start the exam. Students went to their seats and sat down. Attendance of students was checked and question paper were issued. After that, when the bell rang the students started writing the exam.

The headmaster came to Guna, who was standing alone under a walnut tree and gave her exam card, pen and white papers. The address of the school was rubber stamped on the top of the papers. "You sit here and write, Guna" said the headmaster and walked towards an exam room.

Guna sat under the tree. After thinking for a while, she drew a picture of a flower plant on the paper. It was a small plant with five leaves and a flower with six petals at the top. To others, her image appeared blured. They didn't know what lies hidden within those scribblings. After drawing a picture, she got bored. No one to play with. Everyone were writing their exams. It was then, she remembered the tiffin box which she had brought. She opened it and ate patiently. Lemon rice and coconut thuvaiyal. Although she had eaten at home just a while ago, she ate a little now. It's like a game for her.

After eating, she went to the tap to wash her hands and went to every classroom to see where Ramamurthy sir was. He was standing in class 10 and invigilating the students who were writing their exams. When she saw him, she laughed and shouted excitedly, but Ramamurthy sir stopped her at the entrance and said: "Guna, don't come here. The exam is going on. Go and play under the tree!"

She stood outside and watched the examiners inside. Everyone smiled at her and said by sign, "Go, go…" Guna turned around.

Just then, a goat was about to come in through the ruined barbed wire fence of the school garden. Some amaranth in the garden were growing well. Guna ran and chased away the goat. The goat stared at her as if asking her, "Who are you to drive me away?". She picked up a piece of stick that was lying on the ground and raised it up. With hesitation, desperation and disgust, it left. When it went beyond the campus door, she locked the door and came. A lot of pods and fruits were lying under the walnut tree. It was always the other students who crushed them with stones and gave her the pulses. There was no one to help her that today. She picked up one of the red almonds and scraped the skin off with her teeth. It was sweet. Then she gathered every fruit and fruit that had fallen and piled it between the two roots of the tree so that no one could take it.

A few days ago, the cleaner had collected all the fallen leaves from the walnut tree and dumped them in the garbage heap at the backyard. But here, again, there were lot of leaves. Most of them were dry.

Luckily the motor room was open. She went there and brought a broom and a basket and began to sweep. She carried all the leaves. She collected everything in a basket and dumped them in the garbage heap. Then she was about to step on a caterpillar. Caterpillars often come from the walnut trees. But it was a bit too big. She watched the movement of the caterpillar for a while and continued her work.

After putting the leaves into the basket for four times and dumping them in the garbage heap, the place became clean. But again, some leaves had started falling here and there. She was tired. She took the basket and broom and left it in the motor room. The handkerchief near her neck was slightly wet with saliva flowing from the mouth.

After fetching some stones, she played with it, under the tree for a while, she didn't know what to do. She suddenly got up and started dancing her usual dance. It went on for a while, jumping up and down, swinging her legs back and forth and twirling with its arms outstretched. Then she bowed her head as always to salute the compliments at the end of the dance. She waved her hands in the air as if shaking everyones hands.

Just then, a large plastic bag flew through the air and grabbed her leg. It had a picture of a fan printed on it. She took it and threw it in the garbage heap. She took a broken pen from the side and put it into the plastic bag. After walking two steps, she saw the empty water bottle, the chocolate wrappers and the crumpled paper . As she walked, she saw the broken pencil, the broken scale, the written notebook paper, the pieces of bracelet, the hairpins… the bag was half full when she went to the garbage dump. Her back hurt from bending over and she started sweating. Without her knowledge she was drooling.

She came and took water in a tumbler from the water tap and drank it.

The garden flowers were beginning to wilt in the sun. The children did not water them as they were studying hard in the morning. Guna went back to the motor room and brought the bucket. She took water little by little and poured it on the flowering plants. Her dress was wet with water and mud till her knee. She didn't worry about that. She watched in amazement as the wind whipped up the dirt and some feathers nearby.

At that time, some chickens tried to enter the campus gate through the wire bars. Guna quickly ran and chased them. The vegetable cart vendor from the street, stood next to the school gate and shouted loudly, "brinjal…, Raw mango…, Lady's finger…". Guna angrily yelled at him, "Don't shout here, go away!" He did not understand what she was saying, but moved away from the place as no one came to buy.

On her way back Guna noticed the headmaster's room through the window. The vase on his desk was empty. Every morning, the flowerpot will be filled with flowers placed by the children so that the room looks very beautiful. Today is the exam and so no one seems to notice.

She plucked hibiscus, oleander and periwinkle from the garden and put them in the flower vase. Like big children, she also poured a little water. She felt very happy. She looked at the flowers and smiled. whole heartedly, she went and kept the bucket in the motor room and left.

Again, a nuisance arrived. At the kitchen door, a dog sniffed and rolled over dishes which had been washed. food was not cooked on exam days. Without knowing her, the dog had just come through the wire gap of the campus gate. She ran furiously, chased it away and took the vessels and arranged them properly.

That time, she saw a piece of potato lying beside her. It must have slipped off from someone's plate yesterday while providing nutritious food. Otherwise, students who came to the water tap to wash their plates, might have thrown the leftover food.

Guna looked at it and thought for a while. Then she took it. Looking around, the space between the motor room and the water tap seemed ideal. She poked it with a stick, scraped it with her fingernail and dug a small hole there. She put the piece of potato in the hole and covered it with soil and she collected a glass of water and poured it.

The silk handkerchief was half soaked in saliva. Thanvi from class eight came to drink water from the water tap, she grabbed Guna and hugged her, wiped her saliva with the hem of her upper top and hurried away.

As she was taking the drawing paper and the exam card to the headmaster's desk, she saw her father's tricycle approaching the campus door. Slinging her book bag over her shoulder and holding the wire basket in one hand, she ran towards her father with a squeal of joy.

Next day when Guna came to school, the first thing she did was to look at the place where she had sow the piece of potato yesterday.

At that spot, a brand-new plant with five leaves had sprouted. A small blue flower with six petals on top of it! Just like she had drawn on her paper yesterday!

She couldn't control her overwhelming joy. She ran to the science teacher to show the plant. He was still in the examination room, waved his hand, when he saw her, and 'Don't come here!'

She came back and looked at the little plant with kindness and a smile. Then she went to get a basket and a broom to sweep up all the fallen leaves under the tree.

8
Winged Scorpion

Jai and his little sister Thanvi were returning from school by cycle. It started raining out of the blue. Sadly, there was no nearby place to take shelter. Jai was afraid that their books would get drenched in the rain. He was recently given books for class 8 at school.

They both had canvas bags which they were carrying on their backs. There was a chance that the bag could get soaked in the rain and the books to get wet. The rain started pouring heavily. Jai stopped his cycle near the bus stop which was on the way. Thanvi jumped down from the carrier and ran to the bus stop and sat on one of the seats. When Jai came, his cycle fell down because of the strong wind. He went back and lifted it. Then he parked his cycle in a way that it was leaning against the pillar of the bus stand.

Jai got completely drenched in the rain by that time. The bus stop had only a cement roof with few seats. There was no covering on all the four sides. The rain drops entered easily and made them wet. Little Thanvi was shivering. There were raindrops stuck to her hair. Jai took his kerchief from his pant pocket and gave it to his sister. She took it and wiped her face and hands and then she tied it on her head.

One can go home within 10 to 15 by cycle from that bus stand. Jai thought that instead of standing there and getting soaked by the rain, it would be better to go home soon. He sat on his cycle and called Thanvi. She came running and sat on the carrier.

They both got drenched completely when they reached home. Thanvi without delaying, opened their bags and took out all the books. Thanvi could see that the cover of her two books got wet. In one of them was the money she collected from her sixth-grade students for tomorrow's circus program at school. It was ten rupees per person. Luckily, it didn't get wet. As for Jay, only the top edge of some of his books were wet.

Their father has gone to the night shift work. "You should have waited somewhere until the rain stopped" said his mother with concern.

"There was no safe place to take shelter and the rain did not seem to stop any sooner, mom" replied Jai.

Having dried their wet hair and having changing clothes, their mother gave dry ginger coffee to them. Despite of its spicy flavour, Thanvi liked it a lot. After a long time, the rain stopped, Thanvi went to their veranda. She observed the potted plants to see if there were any new flowers. She saw the two snails which were moving in the rose plant. A spider's web on the lower branch of a hibiscus plant hung in the air.

"DON'T STAND IN THE RAIN THANVI, COME IN" ordered her mom in a loud voice.

On hearing her mother, Thanvi went in and sat on the sofa. Beside her, Jai was reading a detective novel from where he left it.

Thanvi started to have a slight headache. She sat comfortably. Her head started pounding. She sneezed a couple of times in between. She sat down with her legs hanging, her head tilted back and her eyes closed. Her body felt like it was burning with fever. She got up and laid on her bed, wrapping herself with the blanket. Her mother thought that she would be usually studying at this time and not sleeping like she was doing now. She came near Thanvi and placed her hand under Thanvi's forehead.

FEVER!!!....

Immediately, her mother opened the box which contained all the essential pills. It seemed like they have ran out of the fever tablet. A few minutes later, her body started shaking. She groaned and turned left and right. She started shivering much. Suddenly her tongue went dry and her breath was hot.

Her mother wrote four to five types of medicine on a piece of paper and gave it to Jai. "Take the money from our cupboard and get the medicines. Come soon. "Said his worried mother. Then she informed his father on the phone. "There is no one to look after my job. I will come early in the morning. Take good care of our Thanvi. Give her some medicine. If the fever does not subside, call Prem and take her to Dr. Srinivasan by his auto," said his father.

Jai left to buy the medicines. The medical shop was two kilometres away from their house. Among the medicines prescribed by his mother, two of them were not available at Razi medicals. That is were they usually buy medicines. Then Jai bought the remaining two medicines, one from Nalwar medicals and one from Bhava medicals and returned home.

It was very dark. The cold wind and the drizzles have not subsided yet. Jai kept the medicines in his pant pocket and pedalled his cycle at high speed. He was sad thinking that he was the reason for Thanvi's suffering. But there was no place to take shelter from the rain. Thanvi had a weak body and she was a scared-cat. Even for little things, she will break down completely. All these thoughts made him worried. He pedalled his cycle as fast as he could. The cold drizzle crashed against his face, chest and hands. He checked whether the medicines were in his pockets.

Jai turned his cycle at the turning that led to his house.

Thanvi's sixth grade class teacher, Abdul Wahab lived there. He was a science teacher. They have to go past his house every day. As they pass the house on his bicycle, Jai and Thanvi have a tremor in their hearts. It is enough to hear his voice from inside the house, they both will obviously get scared. Abdul Wahab was known to be the strict teacher, not only for them, but for all the students in the school. He had a strong influence on the students. If students see him coming from a distance, they would go in opposite direction and hide themselves.

However, he never hit the students nor shout at them. His normal tone of speech sounded like threatening. If he says "hmm" it was considered as a roar, and his "uhm" is considered as a growl. His stiff structure and twisted moustache are enough!!! Then there was an inherent majesty in his walk and gestures.

Mr. Wahab was an excellent teacher. But still, the students will be happy if he does not attend the class. During other teacher's classes, the students' voices can be heard, but the only sound that can be heard during Wahab sir's class is his thunderous voice. Even though the students know the answers to his question, they will be too afraid to speak. They stop out of the fear of getting it wrong.

Jai pedalled his cycle at high speed to get past his house quickly. He passed the house. It was only after he got a little further, he remembered that he saw something shiny lying at the entrance of his house.

Jai stopped his cycle and looked back. The streetlights were not working. The only light on the street was the tube light from Wahab sir's door. The thing lying on the doorway shimmered and moved. The surrounding darkness made it look as if thousands of fireflies were

moving in one place. Jai was surprised. "Has anyone left their diamond jewellery? Or, are they just broken pieces of glass?" Jai wondered.

Jai parked the cycle in a corner. There was a danger that Wahab sir might suddenly open the door and come and see him. But the glittering object attracted him. "WHAT IS THAT?" curiosity gripped him. He moved closer.

It was wriggling. It was a living creature. It looked like scorpion in dark blue. Jai bent a little more and looked closely. It not just looked like a scorpion but a REAL SCORPION!!! It was like a scorpion that was made using cotton. It had, four legs in a side, for a total of eight legs. In pure yellow, it had two big palps in the front. The tail part was pink in colour and the end of the tail was deep red in colour. Like the wings of a butterfly, it had glittering green wings on its flanks. It was the blue dots on the wings that shone so brightly. The entire body of the scorpion shone brightly like velvet. One of its wings was half torn and hanging. "That is the reason why it is lying on the ground throbbing" thought Jai.

He had never seen such a kind of insect ever before. He felt that this weird looking scorpion would be highly poisonous. Its length was approximately more than half an inch. Its thickness would be that of three fingers. Just like how some snakes used to squirt their poison, he was scared that this scorpion would also do so. It was a dangerous species, no doubt about it. It was lying near Wahab sir's house.

What to do if it crawls inside his house. In his house, Wahab sir lived with his wife and his two children. If it bites what will happen to the children! He could not even think about it. He felt pity! They were little ones! Right at that moment he remembered about his sister who is suffering from fever. After that he did not think about anything else. He hoped on his cycle and started to pedal it.

But his heart would not listen to him. The scorpion could hide anywhere outside Wahab sir's house, and bite him when he comes outside… or it could enter his house and hide somewhere inside. It might wait for the right time to attack his wife or children… Oh God! Nothing like that should happen. It would have been fine if he hadn't seen the insect but he had already seen it.

Should he go without preventing the life danger that it would bring? What to do?

He remembered about his sister Thanvi then, therefore he moved forward towards his house.

Silence prevailed everywhere. All he could hear was the sounds of the night bugs. The sky was filled will clouds like smoke and the moon was seen slightly hiding behind them.

Afterwards, suddenly Jai turned his cycle, don't know what he thought, and came stood in the spot where the insect was lying. The shiny insect was shaking it's claws and was dragging a feather which was sticking on the floor, moving forward slowly. Only two steps and then it would reach Wahab sir's door.

On one side Jai was feeling bad and was praying for his sister. He stopped his cycle and went towards the main door. Is this the right thing to do? Should we go and get caught in the hold of this rude man. Jai was confused. Even then he knocked the iron gate. The noise of the knocking seemed a lot in that silence.

No one opened the door. After waiting for a few minutes, he started to knock the door more vigorously. He knocked for five more times. He was startled by the noise he made. 'who is at the door at this time? Do you have brain?' Shouted Wahab sir. What to do now. Should I get mended in some unwanted work? There Thanvi was fainting in fever. His mother was waiting for him to bring the tablets. Is it really necessary? like those thoughts ran through his mind. But he could not got away from there.

Whatever happens let it be. Let Wahab sir come out scold, me or beat me. He decided to bear. Nothing would happen to Thanvi.

Jai with determination opened the lower latch of the door. With the force that he had opened, the left side of the door went and dashed against the wall and stopped.

Jai went inside and knocked the inner door. He continuously knocked for two to three times; something fell down with a force from the nearby mango tree. Maybe a bird or its nest he did not know exactly what it was.

The door was not opened. That house did not have a calling bell either. He got a little bit angry and irritated at Wahab sir.

Again, he started to knock the door. Continuously he knocked for six to seven times. His right palm started to pain. Hearing this the next-door people opened their door, looked outside and again closed it.

Jai didn't understand what to do further. He was standing stunned just like that. Tears sprung up in his eyes when he thought about Thanvi. He touched his pockets which held the tablets.

Silence… only silence prevailed all around. The drizzle was starting to increase. The moon which was seen earlier was nowhere in sight.

Right now, that insect with its shiny body was slowly moving and had reached the door. Jai thought of trying one last time and raised his hand to knock, at the exact moment the door was opened.

Wahab sir peeped outside the door and his face held an angry and irritated expression. His wife and children were standing behind him which can be clearly seen. His face held a kind of expression which screamed ' who have the guts to knock my door'. He came out slowly upon seeing Jai. Jai had a kind of fear which ran from his head to his feet. He did not wait till he was questioned. He hid his fear and started to speak while stuttering.

"Sir, near your door there is a huge insect which looked like a scorpion. Look here sir! It seemed like a highly poisonous one Sir. That's why to alert you I knocked your door sir. Forgive me for disturbing you sir…"

He had no idea about what he spoke. After saying this, he turned around and took his cycle and disappeared in lightning speed.

After he left, Wahab sir observed the insect for sometime. Then he went inside his house and brought a torch light and observed the insect under the light for a long time.

Six months later, one day, a car halted outside the school campus. From the car stepped out the district Education officer and few others. They came suddenly without any prior notice which shocked and surprised the school's principal. He nervously ran to the gate to welcome them. Knowing that the authorities had come, all the teachers came and greeted them.

There was not enough space for everyone who had come to sit in the principal's cabin. Therefore, the principal and the officer sat inside while the others stood outside talking. The helper who was about to get tea for everyone was stopped by the officer who said: "Sir, can you please call Jai who is studying in ninth standard and Wahab sir?".

Within the next few minutes both of them were brought there. Before Wahab sir can greet them, the officer stood up and greeted both of them. Jai who stood next to Wahab sir felt sick in his stomach. Bearing it he stood there, confusedly.

The officer said to the Principal: "This boy Jai who is our student has found a very new species sir. A winged scorpion! The thing that he found, was sent to 'Delhi biological corporation' by Wahab sir asking, "what type of animal that is". After exploring for a long time they have provided a certificate stating that such a kind of animal till now remained undiscovered in the world. Delhi biological corporation had sent this to America for further investigation and even they have confirmed this".

Wahab sir smiled. It was such a rare sight for Jai. He looked like a child when he smiled.

The officer spoke: "From the email that Wahab sir sent, our education minister had received a message from America. I am only here upon his request. In a few days this will be declained through news channel and media. Our school is going to get

worldwide recognition. The reason for this is, this boy Jai and Wahab sir".

The Principal stood up and took Wahab sir's hand in his and shook it. He also hugged Jai. The officer too embraced Jai and patted his cheeks affectionately.

Jai, Wahab sir, and the Principal were told attend the International Science Congress which will be held in Delhi on twenty third June where Jai will be awarded with medal, certificate and even cash prize.

The Officer, Wahab sir and the Principal were speaking further about this with immense happiness. Jai silently sneaked outside and went towards the sixth standard to see his sister Thanvi.

9

The Chicken which fell into the pit

It happened to be a wrost morning for Jai and his sister Thanvi. A chicken had fallen into a pit which was dug in the backyard to construct a well.

The construction work is yet to be completed. The pit was five feet in breath and six feet in depth. Since it was Sunday, the work was paused to be continued the next day. At such a time, the chicken had fallen into the pit!

At first Jai could not understand why the mother hen was making sound while going around the pit, flapping its wings. Its eleven chickens were making 'keech, keech' sounds and were running here and there behind their mother.

Jai ran and saw what the commotion was all about and called his sister: "Thanvi, come here fast, a chicken has fallen into the pit!". Thanvi left the painting of nature that she was doing and came running, "Aiyoo! Chicken!"

She looked into the pit and made a sound which scared the mother hen and the chickens who ran away hearing it, they turned and looked back. The hen stood in front of them and stated its point, "cock, cock… save my child, bring him up…". It also flapped its wings. The chickens also

stood surrounding them as if saying "please save our sibling! we only believe you".

Thanvi ran inside and brought her mother to show her. Then the hen and the chickens surrounded her and made pathetic sounds. Mother who saw inside the pit said, "we will ask your father to take it out once he come home" and left. The important thing for her right at the moment was drying the papads under the sun on a white cloth which laid on the rope bed.

The brother and sister duo did not like the carelessness shown their by mother.

"What if it gets late for father to come, till then should the chicken suffer? Is that right" asked Thanvi furiously at her brother.

Jai felt that whatever she was saying was right. The hen was suffering and can be seen going around the pit while fluttering its wings. The chickens which were running behind the hen were crying.

The chicken inside the pit ran inside in circles making sounds. Now and then it tried to fly up using its small wings. It was a pathetic sight that, it could not fly more than two or three feet.

Jai and Thanvi became so anxious. When Thanvi stood at the edge of the pit and peeped inside it, few stones slipped her feet and feel inside the pit. Thankfully it did not hit the chicken. The mud and dirt fell down and made a sound which scared the chicken which started to shout in fear. The hen which heard the cry of the little one came to peck them both. Thanvi took a stone and shooed it away. Jai warned the hen angrily: "can't you be quiet? We are just trying to help you!". The hen backed off.

Jai ran and went to a nearby Indian tulip tree, broke a branch and brought it. He did not know what to do after reaching the pit. He put the branch down. He ran inside his house, brought some rice and threw them inside and around the pit. The chicken inside saw up and then jumped but did not eat the rice. The chicken which saw this with unbearable sorrow and suffered, "cock, cock…" and sat on the edge of the pit. The other chickens ate the scattered rice.

Thanvi stood worried while fudging with her fingers not knowing how to save the chicken. Again, Jai ran inside his house and brought a small plastic bucket and rope. He tied the rope to the bucket and put it inside the pit. The hen also peeped to see what is happening.

As soon as the bucket touched the bottom of the pit the chicken got scared and stood aloof. Then, it understood that it is not something to be scared of and flew and sat on the edge of the bucket. Then jumped back on the ground. Again, it climbed on the edge and jumped down. At such a critical situation, it found an interesting game and again and again repeated the same happily.

Thanvi who saw this shouted in anger: "Hey, idiot, sit inside the bucket. Only then we can bring you up and save you. Immediately come and sit inside the bucket. Do as we say!".

But the chicken looked up once upon hearing her voice but again continued its play. The moment it sat on the edge Jai tried to pull the bucket up but it suddenly jumped down. Thanvi scolded the chicken while stomping her foot on the floor, "one should either have common sense or should listen to others. What to do when one lacks both?".

The hen like possessed ran here and there and again started to round the pit, shouting. "Don't kill me shouting, just be quiet, we are trying only right" advised Thanvi. It kept quiet for few minutes but again started making sounds. While circling the pit a chicken was about to fall inside the pit but Thanvi pushed it the other side coming in speed of thunder. "Everyone don't fall into the pit! Go and stand that side, donkeys!" she shooed the hen and the chickens. But they went to a certain distance and again came near the pit "cock, cock…".

Martin who was studying in second standard came out of his house which was opposite to Thanvi's house. He saw a cartoon regarding pigs in the television a few days back. He liked it very much. The movie showed 'Daddy pig'; 'Mommy pig' and he started to address people the sameway. Upon seeing him Thanvi shouted: "hey, Martin come here, a chicken has fallen into the pit". Martin came running and peeped inside the pit. "Thanvi pig, what is this chicken pig doing inside the pit?".

Suddenly Thanvi got angry and picked up a stick lying on the ground to strike him. Then she dropped it in the ground and said fiercely: "If you are going to blabber pig 'mig' etc. I'll push you inside the pit".

Jai consoled them: "Don't fight. Let's think on how to save this chicken and bring it out!". Martin accepted it and said "Jai pig what if we tie a rope to that tree, get inside the pit holding it?". Jai felt the urge to slap him. He controlled himself with a lot of difficulty.

Next door Aiysha was returning home after buying vegetables. Thanvi called her: "Hey Aiysha! Come here, the chicken had fallen into the pit!"

Aiysha kept her vegetable bag inside her home and came immediately. She peeped into the pit after escaping from the hen which came to peck her: "Oh, oh! Poor chicken!". Martin then said, "Aiysha pig, don't go near the pit or else you'll fall into it" he warned. Aiysha frowned at him, "if you call me pig once more I'll grind and squash you like a coconut in grindstone" she warned.

Once more Jai tried to save the chicken by putting the bucket down. It was of no use. Aiysha's mother came and called her: "Aiysha, come let's eat!". Thanvi boiled in anger seeing her: "can't you understand anything? What is happening here and what are you talking! A chicken has fall into the pit!"

Normally Thanvi is a calm girl who would not retort back. For Aiysha's mother Thanvi's behaviour appeared weird. She saw Thanvi with wonder and left.

The hen tried to chase away the kids from there. But that did not happen. It sat at a distance with its wings folded. The chickens too stood near it.

Jai, Thanvi and Aiysha thought about it and discussed it. They longed to find a way to save the chicken. To Thanvi that was the most important thing right at the moment. However, if they save the chicken then that would be enough. They can go and eat peacefully.

Aiysha said with enthusiasm: "There, Postman is coming! Let's call and ask him!". Thanvi and Aiysha ran to the postman who had stopped his cycle next door.

"Uncle, a chicken has fallen into the pit. Can you take it out, please…" asked Thanvi with utmost request.

The postman analysed the situation. "We can take it out only with the help of a ladder," saying that he left. They felt disappointed. Next when they asked help from a lady who sold colour powders, she too did the same.

Thanvi felt anxious and her anger increased thinking about their inability. The fear of something happening to the chicken while inside the pit added to her misery. Her head began to pound. Martin said with worry: "it would be nice if we have a ladder pig!".

Nearby houses did not have a ladder. Tahsildar who resided at the house in the street end held an iron stool. It was impossible right then to carry such a weight and place it in the pit. Apart from that, that house would always be locked from inside. If we knock the door a dog from inside will start barking.

The time was ticking. The hen now in anger was walking around the pit. Behind it the chickens followed stumbling. Now there is no sound heard from the pit. The chicken was shivering standing in the same place. Thanvi doubted that if the chicken is feeling drowsy. They were looking intently inside the pit focusing on the chicken. They did not know what was going to happen to it. It sat inside the pit. Now everyone felt tensed. Little by little the temperature was increasing and therefore Thanvi feared that it would become so hot inside the pit.

Murugesan came pushing the vegetable cart while shouting "Buy vegetables, mother, vegetables, spinach, green chillies…" upon seeing the children he too came and peeped inside the pit, "it seems as if the chicken will die!" he said. When Thanvi heard this her anger knew no bounds: "don't you have a little bit of qualms! It is also a life and you're telling that it is going to die! Shut your mouth up and go mind your business!".

Murugesan who did not expect it the least stood startled. He left after a few minutes of mumbling.

The heat increased. The ground started to burn hot. Now the chicken was lying inside the pit. Now and then it raised its head and made sounds.

The hen peeped and mumbled something as if it is gave hope to the chicken. Afterwards, there was no sounds nor any movement from the chicken. With their heart palpitating they intently looked at it and concluded that was all over.

At that time Jai went near the rope bed where his mother had kept the papads for drying. The Mother was not there. He took the cloth and kept it down and took the bed along with him. They then pushed the bed horizontally, and leaned the bed with the support of the wall. Holding Thanvi's hand Jai stepped onto the wooden handle of the bed. Then he slowly got down holding the ropes. They only wavered but did not get cut because they were tied strongly. Little by little he got down, took the chicken in his hand and loudly said: "it is still alive! It opening its mouth! It will get well if we give it water to drink!".

Thanvi, Aiysha and Martin upon hearing the voice felt great relief. A small smile blossomed upon Thanvi's sweating face. "Just like that carry it up brother!" said Thanvi and hurriedly took a coconut shell and filled it with water.

Jai carried the chicken in one of his hands softly and climbed up with the help of other hand slowly. The chicken became tired and lightly opened its mouth. The hen which saw it jumped here and there and suffered. The chickens too made sounds. Aiysha was expecting the moment the chicken would come up.

Jai who reached half the distance held his hands up and said "Thanvi, here take the chicken".

Thanvi with glowing face happily reached out to take it. Aiysha said to Jai as if appreciating him, "very good!" And smiled.

No one would have expected something like that to happen at that time. Between Jai and Thanvi's hands came something which looked as if it dashed their hands strongly! In the shock Thanvi got startled and shouted "Maa!" The chicken was not in Jai's hand, just in fraction of seconds! After a few seconds only did they realise that an eagle has taken it away! With the bubbling anger the hen tried to fly and catch the eagle but it failed. 'Aioo!' said Thanvi and sat on the floor with her hand on her head.

"In the end, the eagle pig has taken away the chicken!" exclaimed Martin.

10
Not Because of Pain

Many months have passed since the school opened after Corona. Yet the restrictions were severe. Students' body temperature was measured and were noted in the morning. Sanitizers were provided to clean their hands. Everyone is required to wear a face mask. Students should sit leaving adequate spaces between them in the class.

Jai was given the job to measure everyone's body temperature and note it. He is in eleventh grade. It is Thanvi's job to spray the sanitizer on the hands of the students and the teachers. All these activities are monitored by the physical education teacher. Thanvi is Jai's sister. She is studying in class 10 in the same school. They both volunteered to do this work.

Jai and Thanvi have to report to the school at 8.30 a.m., to check the temperature and spray the hand sanitizer. They have to put a chair outside and keep the thermometer, sanitizer bottle, and the register and arrange everything. They need to clean the whole place. From the gate to the place of examination, circles should be drawn with bleaching powder at a distance sufficient for a man to stand. When all these works are done, the time will be 9'o clock. After all this work, the teachers and the students will start coming. Slowly one by one.

One Monday, Jai and Thanvi prepared everything and were waiting. The principal was in his room. The students started coming one by two. They stood in the circles drawn at a distance. Jai placed the thermometer on each one's forehead, then measured and noted the temperature. Then Thanvi sprayed sanitizer on their hands. After the sanitizer has been sprayed, the students rubbed both of their palms together. The physical education teacher was standing beside them and supervised whether everything is happening properly.

Every student has their own way of showing their hands to get the sanitizer. Some of them will show both of their palms well spread. Some hold out only one hand. While the others pretend to cup their hands like they are drinking water from the tap. There are those who hold out and raise their hands as if they are asking God for a boon. It is interesting for Thanvi to see all this.

Malathi, studying in the sixth standard, came. After her, it is Mallika of the tenth standard. Then Ramu, Rajesh, Pudhiyavan, Kala, Thara, Mohana…. everyone stood in the circle and got the sanitizers.

Thanvi was so shocked to see the widespread hands of Gopika!!! There was a big cut on her left hand below the thumb! The blood was clotted in the wound. It seemed as if the cut was made by a sickle or a knife.

Gopika closes her hand and pulls back as she felt that Thanvi has been looking at her hand, stunned. She shifted her school bag to her left hand and showed her the right hand. Thanvi felt that something is off and she understood, then sprayed some drops of sanitizer on that hand.

Gopika and Thanvi belong to the same class. These days, they are not talking to each other. But they used to be close friends. The Department of Posts had announced a district level drawing competition. The topic of the competition for students was "GIRL CHILDREN' SAFETY". Thanvi and Gopika finished their drawings and sent them through their principal. Gopika is very

well skilled in using colours and drawing. There was not single person in the school who was not surprised to see her talents in painting at such a young age. Even the twelfth-grade students would come and ask her to draw the scientific pictures. During festival season, she would draw greeting cards for many. Her paintings of the landscapes, and the portrait of the great leader Kamaraj has been framed and kept in her classroom. Do you know what she drew for the painting competition???

"Many hands were joined together in circle, like the Sun, in the middle of which a girl walks with a school bag on her back."

With precise lines and an attracting colour scheme, the painting was very beautiful and everyone in the school liked it a lot. Even Saroja, who cooks nutritious food, saw it and said to her, "Tell your mother to get rid of the evil eyes, you've drawn so well!!!!" Everyone firmly believed that this drawing will get the first prize. They even congratulated Gopika in advance for it.

Generally, Thanvi does not have interest in drawing. She prefers writing essays. Some of her essays have been published in children's magazines. Chief among them is the essay about the extinct Toto bird, which was published in the Thulir magazine.

The daily newspaper comes to her house. After her dad finished reading it, Jai and Thanvi used to read it. From time to time, there were news of the girls being sexually harassed.

Thanvi's heart hurts when she reads such things happening to girls. She feels a pain that is unbearable and her eyes fills with tears. At such times, she loses faith in the world and in people. She is filled with fear and frustration. She wanted to write an article about these atrocities which are disgraceful to the human race. So, she has gathered the cuttings of the reports regarding this.

Thanvi has read the book, "Marappachi sonna Ragasiyam" written by the children's writer, S. Balabharathi, from her school library. In that book, an old man tries to misbehave with a girl, and the story is about how they punish the man. The book talks about the good touch and bad touch. According to Thanvi, this book must be read by all sections of the society and the girls. She recommended it to many of her friends. Few of them have read the book and talked with her, filled with a satisfaction that they have learned something essential for life. After reading that book, Thanvi felt a sense of caution. She sadly realized that there are many dangerous people in this world. This book has taught her a lot more about the safety of the girls.

When Thanvi saw the notice of the drawing competition on the notice board, an idea immediately flashed in her mind. She decided at that very moment that she should take part in that competition.

Her drawing for the competition looked like this:

There was a land that is dried and cracked. In between the cracks, newspaper's cuttings about girls being sexually harassed were cut and pasted. From a big crack in the ground, a girl's hand with bangles reaches towards the Sky. Below it, she had written a slogan stating, "SAVE GIRL CHILDREN", in bold red colour.

The lines and the colours used in that painting was not that great. It looked like a baby's drawing. Gopika looked at this painting, and said, "It looks like a child's scribbling," with a sarcastic smile. Thanvi felt a bit ashamed.

Many people who saw her drawing commented that, "What is this? You've drawn like a child? You could have drawn well like Gopika, couldn't you?? Some looked at her drawing with disgust and some with indifference.

Thanvi felt like crying. She was greatly confused and hesitated whether to give this to the principal and ask him to send it or not. Finally, she went to the art teacher. He was the only one who was genuinely happy after seeing her drawing.

"This drawing talks about an important matter in a serious tone" he said. And also, he added that the more he see this drawing, the sadder it is.

Worried Thanvi, shyly asked the teacher, "Is the drawing not good sir? Does it look like a child's art??" The art teacher got up and opened the cupboard near them. He took a large sketchbook from the cupboard and showed it to her. Many world-renowned artists have drawn and coloured as it was done by a little child. Thanvi was surprised and felt happy when she saw all of them. The art teacher said:

"You don't have to draw like anyone. Everyone has to draw in their own way. You have to draw according to what your heart feels. Use all the colours you like. You don't even have to worry about what others think about your drawing. Do you like your own drawing?? That is the only thing that matters."

"In 1946, art exhibitions were organized in Britain and France. The drawings displayed were all done by the children. The world-famous artist, Picasso was invited to inaugurate the exhibition. Picasso was very much fond of the children's drawings. Do you know what he said then?? 'When I was a child, I used to practice like my predecessor, Artist Raphael. Then it took me ten years to draw like a child.'

"When Picasso was a child, people used to tell him to draw like Raphael. As a result, Picasso started drawing like him. Afterwards he realized, 'Alas!!! a mistake has happened. I should draw only like a child, Shouldn't I??' But he forgot how to draw like a child. He later had to learn to draw like a child and it took him ten years. So, there is nothing wrong with drawing like a child. It is too good. You go and submit your drawing confidently!!!"

Thanvi felt extremely happy after hearing what her art teacher said. She gained confidence through his support. She submitted her drawing to her principal to be sent to the competition.

The principal looked her drawing closely, then he saw her with pity. "Why do you have to do this? Isn't Gopika there to draw in our school?? Then why have you scribbled something and come? I am ashamed to even send this. But what can I do? I must send it, mustn't I?? Okay, now you can go!!" said the principal.

Thanvi returned with a broken heart. She felt that she should get her drawing back. But the words said by her art teacher made her to feel strong.

After a few weeks, everyone in the school was shocked when the results of the drawing competition were published in the magazine.

Thanvi got the first place for her drawing. Let alone the first three prizes, Gopika did not get a single one of the ten consolation prizes. The Art teacher praised her whole heartedly.

Everyone was sad over the fact that Gopika's very talented drawing did not win the prize. So, Thanvi's success was shadowed and was not given much importance. Only eight out of the twenty teachers wished her outwardly. Out of the thirty thousand rupees she got as a gift, she went with her family and donated twenty-five thousand rupees to 'Devamalar School'. That is a primary school for the deaf and mute children. Her plan is to use the remaining five thousand rupees to buy good books for her school library.

. . . .

It was only after that incident that Gopika started distancing herself from Thanvi. At one point, she stopped talking with her altogether. Gopika, who sat in the third bench beside Thanvi, moved back to the fifth bench and sat with Chandra.

She could not bear her defeat. Disappointment and shame were continuously raging in her heart. "I would never lose in a drawing competition. How many drawings have I drawn!! Last month when Tamil teacher retired, the principal asked not anyone but me to draw a greeting card and then framed it and presented her!! Above everything! I have won the three painting competitions held at the district level and have given the trophies to the school, Haven't I?? I have been drawing since I was in the third standard!!! And I lost to someone who does not even know how to draw??" she kept thinking such things and was burning in rage. Whenever she saw Thanvi, anger rose in her heart like a big raising wave.

Thanvi also understood her mood and stayed away from Gopika. Sitting at the back desk, Gopika would make fun of Thanvi, in a way that she could hear. She would imitate the way Thanvi walks and talks to the other students. Gopika even spits furiously when Thanvi walks past her on the ground. These days, Thanvi is scared to see Gopika. She avoided going near her.

However, one day the physical education teacher drew a white line on the ground, at a place on the field. Behind that line, he made the tenth standard students to stand one after the other according to their height. This is the preparatory work for the sport, Shot-put. As per his order, Thanvi had to stand in front of Gopika. Thanvi had no other choice but to obey his order. After making everyone stand, he could see that Mallika was standing on the line. The teacher blew the whistle and ordered, " Everyone!! Take two steps back and stand behind the line!!" When those who are standing in the front took two steps back, Thanvi also naturally took two steps back, without being aware that Gopika was standing without taking a step back. Thanvi, who moved back, unknowingly bumped into Gopika and trampled her foot. At the very moment, Gopika moved back and slapped Thanvi's back with a SHH..." Who could have expected this to happen? Poor Thanvi stumbles and falls, but managed to stand holding Malini's back, who standing in front of her. Malini looked behind and asked her what happened. Then, as Thanvi did not reply, she turned again. The students who were standing behind also did not know what has happened.

That placed burned as if someone had poured a spoon of fire over it, extreme pain she left. For few minutes it seemed as if she has lost her vision.

She left the line and slowly walked near the library and sat in the steps with her head bowed. She used her palms to hide her face.

Physical education teacher hurriedly came near Thanvi. Before he could reach her, Thanvi stood up and said "Nothing sir. Just a slight headache!".

PE teacher asked: "Did you eat in the morning?"

"I came only after eating sir"

"I think it may be due to the suns heat. Okay, okay. You go to the class".

The pain due to the slap on her back did not even reduce single bit. With tears in her eyes Thanvi said "I will go home sir. I cannot bear it…"

PE teacher looked at Thanvi for few minutes then left for the headmaster's room to ask for permission and said after coming back,

"Okay. Headmaster said that you can leave. But don't go alone. He said to take your brother along with you".

Thanvi went to her classroom to take her schoolbag and came out. She went and stood outside Jai's classroom. Inside math's class was going on. Upon seeing Thanvi Jai stoop up, took his teacher's permission and came out. Jai started to panic after seeing sorrow and tears in her eyes.

"What Thanvi did you get fever?"

"No, brother. Just headache. Headmaster told me to take you home along with me".

Suddenly Jai turned and went inside his class, informed his Math's teacher regarding this, took his school bag and came out.

Thanvi while sitting behind Jai on the cycle, thought only about Gopika. She had gone to Gopika's house several times. Gopika along with her father and mother resides in a small house located in between the fields. Gopika's father and mother rented the place from its owner and does farming for a living. There only for the first time Thanvi has seen huge mongoose.

Gopika knows everything right from ploughing to harvesting. She has kept all her paintings in a wooden suitcase in her house.

Thanvi would be surprised seeing them." How can she draw so beautifully" often Thanvi would wonder. Few times Thanvi have had lunch there. Gopika's mother would serve her simple, yet delicious food. She still remembers the taste of hot rice served with curd, oil fried brinjal gravy and amla pickle. Backside Gopika's house there is a small vegetable garden to fulfil the family's needs.

Both of them together goes to collect Java plum. They have also picked a lot of date fruits. After plucking the custard apple and collecting them in a basket, while coming back Thanvi's leg slipped and she fell into the field. Thank the goodness no harm was done. Catching the hen from the hills and locking them up would be challenge for both of them.

Gopika had pleasure of plucking the henna leaves, making them into paste and applying them on Thanvi's hands. She had the habit of collecting a variety of feathers and kept them in a box made of palm leaves, she gifted them to Thanvi.

Seeing their friendship there were people who used to be happy for them and also those who burned in jealousy in school. Whenever Gopika used to come to Thanvi's home her father would tell her, "Just complete your twelfth. Ill join you in Kumbakkonam arts college".

Did Gopika forget everything?

Jai using his legs stopped the cycle and said, "Get down, we have reached home" that's when Thanvi came out of her thoughts and got down.

Thanvi did not go to school the following two days. The headache did not go. She also had little nauseous feeling. Thanvi thought that this would be the cause of sudden startlement she got due to the slap. Whenever Thanvi thought about the slap she felt as if a caterpillar was crawling on her back.

On the third day, after Thanvi went to school, she did not find one of her slippers in its place in the afternoon. Everyone slippers were there safely in its kept place but only one of hers were missing. Thanvi and Jai searched the surrounding thoroughly but couldn't find it. At last, when Jai looked up in tiredness, something red on the roof of the staff room caught his eyes. Upon getting suspicious of it being Thanvi's slipper Jai informed the watchman. He brought a ladder from the store room. When they climbed up and saw it was Thanvi's slipper as suspected. It was covered in the leaves shed by a tree.

Who would have thrown it there? Jai did not know. But Thanvi knew but she did not even breathe a word about it.

After a few days Thanvi's English book and math's book was missing. When she asked her classmates, everyone said that they don't know. Then, she could understand who did it. When she searched for them, she found her English book in the dustbin behind the toilet in a torn condition. Behind the tank in a bush, she found her math's book in a terrible condition.

One day, when she took her pen to write, she found the nib in a broken condition. One evening while she was going home sitting behind Jai in cycle, a person coming in motorbike behind them stopped them and said: "Child, your book has fallen down, see".

Jai stopped the cycle and ran to take the book but before he could reach it a cars wheel ran over the book. Thanvi removed her bag only to find the downside of it being torn.

Jai who saw it was furious. "Who did this? Do you doubt someone? Again and again, Jai asked her. "It would have torn by getting struck in something brother," said Thanvi.

"It's not like that, it is due to a blade cut! Who would have done this? The reason was unknown to Jai. Let's ask dad to speak regarding this with Headmaster…"

Have a little patience brother. Till we find who did this, be quiet" Thanvi stopped her brother.

Next day evening when they started home from school, Jai's cycles back wheel was punctured. He did not understand anything. When both of them parked the cycle in the morning it was fine. Now there is a nail in the wheel. Jai with confusion pulled the nail, threw it and started pushing the cycle. Jai felt that someone is doing all these wantonly. "Who would be that, that too someone from our school who would behave so cheaply?" with great annoyance and anger while muttering he came pushing the cycle. The mechanic shop is in far distance. Thanvi walked behind him in thoughts with her head bowed. Things like this continued to happen. Everyday Thanvi went to school with the fear of what is awaiting her on that particular day.

Short white path with bends was seen. Next path started at the ending of one path. Thanvi did not know the route. She did not understand the direction. She ran furiously so that she can come out of the illusionary white place. She saw many watersheds sized pathways in between which was leading into big pathways. Every path was combined with the rest and was like a puzzle which was highly confusing. She ran with determination her breathe increasing by second to escape the place no matter what come. She fell down at the meeting of paths. She again got up spun around and started running. Only small and big paths were seen in bends. Who can she ask for help in that place? Her throat got parched. She was drenched in her sweat. Her thirst was so that she could drink up an ocean. It seemed as if a water reservoir was there in a distance. Thanvi ran along that direction. Yes! There was a lake there. But it was a red lake! Blood filled lake! On the bank of the lake, few unknown insects were crawling. Thanvi froze in her place due to fear. She starred at the lake. Right then…Right then… The pathways started to narrow and narrow and become the fingerprints of a palm. The blood lake became a small cut at the side of that palm. Here, Gopika is showing her wounded hands to Thanvi for hand sanitizer. Suddenly upon realization she took her hand back and showed her other hand to Thanvi.

Thanvi fell down in shock at this point in her dream. Her dress was drenched in sweat. In the lamp light, the wall clock showed early morning three. She went to the kitchen to drink some water and then came back and lied down. She could not sleep. Thanvi was spending each second yearning for the morning dawn to break through.

Thanvi's aunts house is in half kilometer from her house. Her aunt is working as a nurse in the government hospital. She saw Thanvi, when she was ready to start for her work in the scooter. With bag and school uniform walked Thanvi hurriedly upon seeing her aunt and reached her.

It was a wonder for her aunt. She did not understand why Thanvi is there instead of going to school in the morning. Thanvi said something to her upon coming near her. Immediately her aunt went inside the house took some things and kept them in her hand bag and came out. Thanvi sat behind her aunt and both left.

It was late when she reached the school. Classes were started. The headmaster was shocked upon seeing Thanvi coming to school with her aunt. He knew her aunt. When his wife was affected with corona, she was admitted in the government hospital. Till his wife got better and came home, the one who took care of her was Thanvi's aunt.

He stood up and welcomed her happily: "come, sister. It's been days since we met. How are you?"

"I'm good sir. How is your wife?"

Headmaster with a bit of worry said: "there is no problem now, sister. She has improved. But little tiredness is there."

"I have given a food chart right. Eat according to that, it will be enough. She will improve. Sir, can you call Gopika who is studying in Thanvi's class? She had hurt her hands it seems. Thanvi is worried that there will be an infection. That's why I came here to give her an anti-septic injection and treat her wounds.

"Is it so, sister! Thanks a lot!" said headmaster who looked at Thanvi with a kind smile and said to the helper: "Bring Gopika who is studying 10th standard"

After that headmaster and Thanvi's aunt spoke for few minutes.

Gopika did not understand why the headmaster is calling her. Because of that she came there with a lot of fear and hesitance. When she saw Thanvi in headmaster's room her heart dropped! She shivered thinking Thanvi has brought someone to complain about her. With fear she thought how to refuse, if Thanvi complains about her. With ticking minute her fear increased.

But nothing happened like she thought. Aunt went near her, hugged her and saw her palms.

"How did you get hurt dear?"

Gopika did not expect the kind of love the aunt's voice held. After being hesitant for few seconds, she said:" I went with my mother to harvest the crops, cut myself with the sickle".

"Adadaa… Is it paining dear!" when aunt asked, Gopika eyes got filled with tears. She shook her head in "Yes".

Aunt with love caressed her hair and said:" Don't worry. The cut seems big. It should not be left open. Infection will occur and the wound will get bigger. It should be kept clean till it heals. I will give you tablets for two days and give you an injection. Apply this ointment at night before you go to sleep. The pain will fade away. The cut will heal very soon".

Aunt dressed and treated Gopika's wounds with great care. After that she took an ointment, applied it on the wound and pressed cotton upon it and struck the band aid to keep it in place. Then she prepared to give an injection. Upon seeing tears in Gopika's eyes, Thanvi came and stood beside her and said, "Don't be scared. It will feel like ant bite only" and held Gopika's shoulders.

"Aunt, inject her without giving her pain" hearing Thanvi say, "okay, okay. Don't I know…" smiled her aunt.

Gopika held Thanvi's hands tightly when she was injected. Tears fell from her eyes without her knowledge.

That, was not because of the pain.